Little Quack

Lauren Thompson   pictures by Derek Anderson

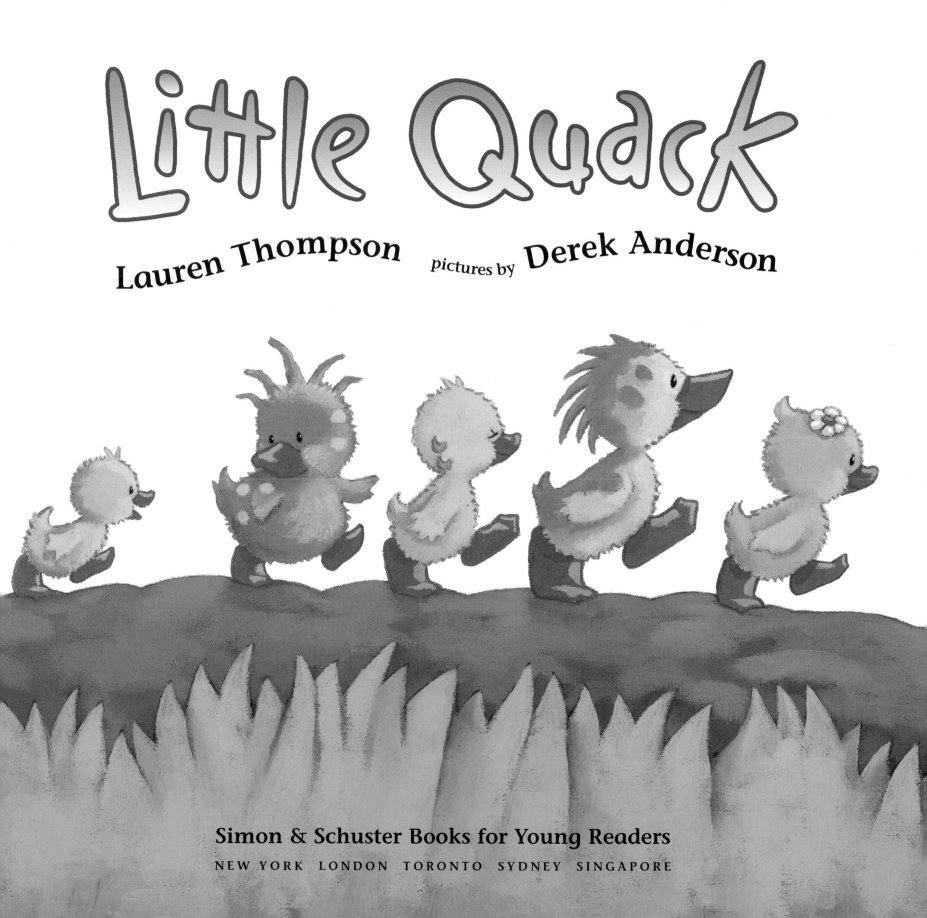

Simon & Schuster Books for Young Readers

NEW YORK LONDON TORONTO SYDNEY SINGAPORE

Mama Duck had five little ducklings, Widdle, Waddle, Piddle, Puddle, and Little Quack. They all lived together in a nice, soft nest.

But even Mama's littlest duckling was not so little anymore. "It's time to leave the nest," she said one day.

"Come, little ducklings," Mama called.
"Paddle on the water with me."
The five little ducklings squeezed close in the nest.
"No, Mama, no!" they cried. "We're too scared!"
"You can do it," Mama said. "I know you can."

COUNT ALONG WITH THE QUACK-U-LATOR!

NO DUCKLINGS IN THE POND

All at once, Widdle felt very brave.
She jumped into the pond—

SPLISH!

"Look!" she cried. "Look at me!"

Now four little ducklings snuggled close in the nest.
"Come, little ducklings," Mama called again.
"Paddle on the water with me."
"No, Mama, no! We're too scared!" cried Waddle,
Piddle, Puddle, and Little Quack.
"You can do it," Mama said. "I know you can."

= 1

ONE DUCKLING IN THE POND

Then Waddle felt very brave.
He plopped into the pond—

SPLASH!

"Hooray!" he cried. "Hooray for me!"

Now three little ducklings clung close in the nest.
"Come, little ducklings," Mama called again.
"Paddle on the water with me."
"No, Mama, no! We're too scared!" cried Piddle,
Puddle, and Little Quack.
"You can do it," Mama said. "I know you can."

🦆 + 🦆 = **2**

TWO DUCKLINGS IN THE POND

Then Piddle, for a moment, felt very brave.
She wiggled into the water—

SPLOOSH!

"It's fun!" she cried. "It's lots of fun!"

Now two little ducklings cuddled close in the nest.
"Come, little ducklings," Mama called again.
"Paddle on the water with me."
"No, Mama, no! We're too scared!" cried Puddle
and Little Quack.
"You can do it," Mama said. "I know you can."

THREE DUCKLINGS IN THE POND

At last, Puddle felt very brave too.
He leaped into the water—

SPLOSH!

"Wait!" he cried. "Wait for me!"

That left just one little duckling in the nest—
just one Little Quack.

"Come, little duckling!" Mama called once more.
"Paddle on the water with me."
"No, Mama, no!" cried Little Quack. "I'm
scared! I'm just too scared!"
"You can do it," Mama said.
"We know you can!" said Widdle, Waddle,
Piddle, and Puddle.

FOUR DUCKLINGS IN THE POND

Little Quack looked at the water.
He sniffed the water.
He touched the water with his foot.
Could he do it? Did he dare?

Suddenly, Little Quack felt just brave enough.
He closed his eyes. Then—

SPLOSH!

—into the water he plunged.
"I did it!" he cried. "I really did it!"
"I always knew you could," Mama said.

Then off they went, five little ducklings proud as can be—Widdle, Waddle, Piddle, Puddle, and brave Little Quack.

🦆 + 🦆 + 🦆 + 🦆 + 🦆 = 5

FIVE DUCKLINGS IN THE POND!

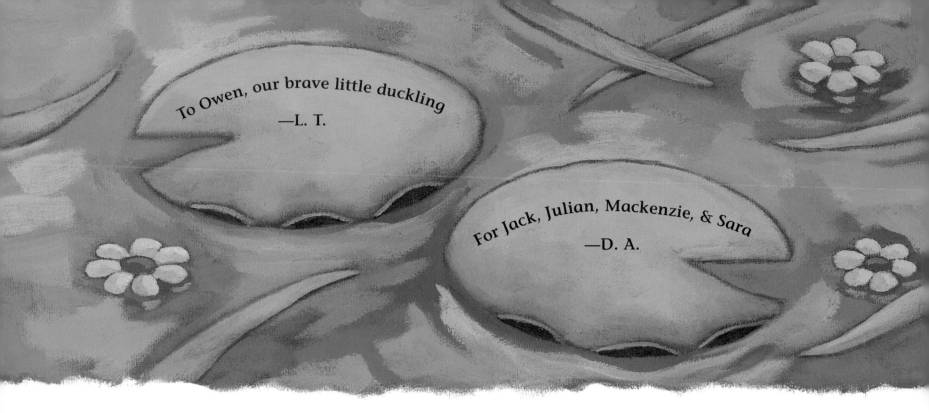

To Owen, our brave little duckling
—L. T.

For Jack, Julian, Mackenzie, & Sara
—D. A.

Special thanks to Muriel Lafferty, District 2 Math Staff Developer based at P.S. 158 in Manhattan, for her thoughtful insight.

SIMON & SCHUSTER BOOKS FOR YOUNG READERS
An imprint of Simon & Schuster Children's Publishing Division
1230 Avenue of the Americas, New York, New York 10020
Text copyright © 2003 by Lauren Thompson
Illustrations copyright © 2003 by Derek Anderson
All rights reserved, including the right of reproduction in whole or in part in any form.
SIMON & SCHUSTER BOOKS FOR YOUNG READERS is a trademark of Simon & Schuster.
Book design by Greg Stadnyk
The text for this book is set in Stone Informal and 99.
The illustrations for this book are rendered in acrylic on canvas.
Manufactured in China
8 10 9
Library of Congress Cataloging-in-Publication Data
Thompson, Lauren.
Little Quack / Lauren Thompson ; illustrated by Derek Anderson.—1st ed.
p. cm.
Summary: One by one, four ducklings find the courage to jump into the pond and paddle with Mama Duck, until only Little Quack is left in the nest, trying to be brave.
ISBN 0-689-84723-8
[1. Ducks—Fiction. 2. Animals—Infancy—Fiction. 3.
Courage—Fiction.] I. Anderson, Derek, ill. II. Title.
PZ7.T37163 Li 2003
[E]—dc21   2002005567